The Door

John Holt

Phoenix Publishing – Essex - UK

CONDITIONS OF SALE

John Holt has asserted his right under the Copyright, Designs and Patents Act 1998 to be identified as the author of this work.

British Library Cataloguing in Publication Data.

A CIP catalogue record for this book is available from the British Library

Printing History

Originally published in May 2021. This Large Print Edition was published by Phoenix, Essex, UK, in June 2023

PREFACE

The story that follows is totally fictitious. It is a story, nothing more and nothing less. All places and persons included in the story are totally imaginary, and any similarity to actual persons alive or dead, is totally co-incidental, and unintentional.

* * *

I am grateful to Lauren Ridley, Cherryloco Jewellery for allowing me to base the Phoenix logo on her design.

John Holt

Chapter One
1st January 1891
The Lansdown School Fire

Lansdown Industrial School was a three storey building on the edge of Hampstead Heath. It was founded in 1819, by wealthy philanthropist, Henry Lansdown. His noble aim was to provide a free education, and provide opportunity, to boys of a working class background. Education, and opportunity which, up to that time, had been denied them. There were five hundred and twenty-five boys registered at the school. Many of them were orphans, and several had parents residing in the Workhouse, or, worse, prison.

With the approach of Christmas, the majority of the boys, the fortunate ones, had gone home for the holiday. However, for a variety of reasons, eighty two boys remained at the school, together with six of the teachers, who had volunteered their services. To the Head Master, it was considered important for the teaching to continue. An opinion not altogether shared by the boys. Nonetheless, everyone was looking forward to celebrating the holiday season. To that end, a number of functions had been arranged, including a pantomime, and a fireworks display.

The celebrations were, however, soon to be disrupted by tragedy.

* * *

It was just twenty minutes after midnight when the first signs of a fire were noticed. The bells ringing in the New Year had ceased some while ago, and the last "Happy New Year" had been called out. The boys were now safely tucked up in their beds, and fast asleep. Silence fell. Apart from a gentle breeze rustling the leaves in the trees, and the tick of the clock on the staircase, there wasn't a sound.

Ben Saintly, a railway worker, had recently finished a long day, and was wearily making his way home. He was looking forward to a well-earned rest, and two days away from the railway. As he walked along The Grove, he noticed a redness in the sky. He thought of the old saying concerning a red sky at night, and the promise of good weather to come. It seemed that he was due some good weather for his two day break. As he continued walking he suddenly could smell smoke, and began coughing. It was then that he realised the colouration in the sky had nothing to do with the weather. It was due to a fire, a big fire. His first thoughts was that it was the nearby forest that was ablaze. As he moved closer and closer to the fire he was shocked to see that it wasn't the forest at all. It was the Lansdown Industrial School. He began running, breathing hard, anxious to sound the alarm, and offer assistance where he could.

"Telegraph, London, 3rd January 1891 .....The peaceful suburb of Hampstead was the scene of a sad calamity at an early hour of New Year's Day, when twenty-four boys, and a number of teachers, lost their lives by fire at the Lansdown Industrial School, a large institution at which between 500 and 600 poor children receive free education. It appears that the poor scholars were enjoying the Christmas Season to the best of their ability. On the afternoon before the tragedy a large party of the elder boys had been to the

theatre to see the pantomime, while a treat had been arranged for the younger children on New Year's Day. The school was gaily decorated, and the poor children went to bed on the last night of the year in eager anticipation of the pleasures which the next day was to bring forth."

* * *

Miss Bradley, the school matron was sound asleep in her room on the first floor. She was aroused by the smell of smoke, and the sound of crackling timbers. She got up, and went into the corridor, and then continued on down the stairs. As she reached the bottom of the staircase, she could see the smoke coming from the top of the partition between a small kitchen area, and the main corridor. She immediately ran back and raised the alarm, by sounding the bell located on the staircase.

"Public Inquiry, Statement by Miss Bradley, Matron, 12th January 1891.... I rang the bell on the staircase, and called up all the other officers. This was about twenty minutes past twelve. Mrs Taylor ran up the stairs and got the keys from the officer who kept them, while I rang the bell. Then we both ran downstairs, and unlocked the dining-hall door. She ran to wake the Head Master, Dr. Shutt, while I ran to find Mr. Lyons. By the time I got back all of the teachers had been aroused."

The sound of the alarm had roused several of the teachers, who had hastily joined the Matron. One of them picked up a fire extinguisher, and endeavored to put out the flames but the smoke forced him back. Within a very short time the fire in the kitchen area had taken hold and was beginning to spread to the curtaining close by. Within minutes the flames were shooting high, and attacking the ceiling timbers. Smoke billowed upwards, through the floor structure, into the dormitories on the floor above.

"Public Inquiry, Statement by Mr. Lyons, German Teacher, 12th January .... Miss Bradley came to find me. By the time I got to the stairway, every officer in the building had come on the scene within a few moments of the alarm being given. Nothing more could have been done, and the utmost was done to save the boys. We have passed through a dreadful night,

and one which we shall never forget so long as we live. My deepest sympathy goes out to those who have lost loved ones in this tragic event."

A telephone call was put through to the local firefighter volunteers, some six miles away. It was to be twenty-five minutes before the horse drawn fire engine arrived at the school, by which time the fire had taken hold. It was not long before the entire east wing of the school was ablaze. The night sky was lit up for miles around. The flames rose high into the air, and the acrid smoke was overpowering.

A number of teachers, including Mr. Lyons, and Mr. Aldridge, had gone to the dormitories, to rescue the children sleeping there, peacefully unaware of the impending danger. However, the outer door was locked and had to be burst in, and on entering the rooms they found most of the boys in bed apparently dazed by the smoke, which filled the room.

"Telegraph, London, 3rd January .... The officers in charge of the dormitories, who alone, with the exception of the Head Master, had keys which will open the various sleeping rooms and wards, were appraised of their danger, and the work of rescuing the children commenced. In the meantime, however, the fire was making dangerous progress and spreading rapidly."

The work of rescuing the boys was both a dangerous and laborious one. There was a secondary access to these dormitories by an outside staircase. However the door leading to the staircase was locked. Alec Aldridge, made his way up the staircase, from the outside, to the dormitory at the top of the landing. When he tried the door, it would not open. He pulled and pushed, until eventually the door was forced open. The room was already full of smoke, and he could hardly see any of the boys inside. He rushed first to the door leading down to the dining hall, but the smoke on the landing was so dense that he had to turn back. He then rushed back to the external staircase, calling to the boys to follow him, and driving some on in front.

Meanwhile, Mr. Lyons attempted to ascend a staircase leading to one of the other dormitories but was stopped for a time by a dense and pungent cloud of smoke which every moment increased in volume. By crawling on his hands and knees he reached the door of the dormitory. He shouted to the boys but received no answer, and then overcome by the smoke he fell down the stairs. Quickly recovering himself, however, he again attempted the extinction of the flames. He helped some of the boys out and when he reached the bottom of the stone staircase he found that the outer door had already been forced open from the outside, and he lead the boys out and away from the building.

"Telegraph, London, 3rd January .....The boys were quickly roused, and escaped by the windows and doors. Some, however, were too stupefied by the smoke or fear to move and were suffocated in their beds. In all 82 boys were

sleeping in the dormitories, and of those 58 were rescued alive, though half choked, the remainder being suffocated before the rescuers could reach them. The boys themselves knew nothing of the beginning of the mischief. A reporter who questioned those who had been rescued was told that some were aroused by the coughing of comrades, and jumped out of bed. Many not realising what was happening, and half asleep returned to their warm bedclothes again, and now lie among the dead on the infirmary floor. One boy even is said, when told of the fire, to have answered, "Nonsense, they are only getting ready for the pudding."

"One or two boys in the lower dormitory jumped out upon the

window ledges, and others were dragged out by their brothers or companions. One boy, named Jones heard another boy cough, woke up, leaped out of bed, and went to look for his little brother. The little brother insisted on putting on his socks before he left the ward, and fell down on the floor never to rise again. Jones began to choke too, but was hauled out into the fresh air.

One boy, sturdy, but not big, came out of the smoke dragging an urchin by each hand, and heard a lad named Jack say he would go back for Tommy. He said, "I am going to give my life up," and went. "I am going back, too," was the statement of another boy presently, who knew by this time that Jack, alas, was amongst the silent ones in the Infirmary. These were sample remembrances amongst the saved, and it is clear that amongst the lads during this horrible trial there were many examples of the real hero. It is very probable that, in the half dazed state of being roused, some boys were suffocated while fumbling for their clothes, and one body, indeed, proved this. The poor lad had succumbed on the floor with only one trouser leg, which he had managed to get on. The scene in the infirmary when the parents arrived to identity the young children's bodies was most touching, many poor mothers being almost prostrated by grief when they saw their little child lying as if asleep."

* * *

The subsequent official investigation was held a few days later, on the 12th of January. It was determined that the fire had started in a small kitchen area, on the ground floor. The cause of the fire was considered to be due to some embers falling from the fire grate, and setting the adjacent rug alight.

Subsequently adjacent curtaining caught fire. The fire soon took hold, and quickly spread. It burnt through the ceiling of the ground floor, and smoke quickly enveloped the dormitories in the floors above. By the morning, twenty-four children and five teachers had died, including one teacher, who had only joined the staff a few days previously. Fifty-eight of the boys were safely rescued.

As for the building, it was totally destroyed. All that remained of the building were some smouldering embers, some charred timbers, and .... a door.

* * *

Chapter Two
5th April 2021 – The Door

David Ashby pulled his coat tightly around him. The weather had suddenly turned quite cold, with a biting northerly wind. He was beginning to wonder if it had been such a good idea to take a walk in the country, after all. He looked up at the sky. It had clouded over and threatened rain. He shook his head, and started to smile. *So much for the warm weather that had been forecast,* he muttered. Although why, with modern methods, they couldn't get a simple thing like a weather forecast correct, was something of a mystery.

So be it, he said. He decided to cut his walk short. He would continue until he had reached The Door, and then he would turn around and head for home.

The Door had become something of a local landmark. Known simply as the door, it was known for miles around. Over the years it had become a popular meeting spot. It had also become something of a marker used when giving directions to someone. Many stories had arisen regarding the door, and its origins. Local children would play tag around the door. Each child would take delight in daring the others to see who would approach the door the closest, and who, if any of them would have the courage to operate the door knocker, or try to open the door. Occasionally, one of the children would use the knocker, and then quickly run away.

* * *

Ashby looked across the forest clearing, at the old door, and smiled. That same old door he had first seen twenty-five years or more previous. It didn't matter how many times he had seen it before, it always seemed somehow new to his eyes. It never changed, and it always intrigued him. *Why was it there anyway?* He wondered. More to the point, how was it there? Who put it in that position? It was just a solitary door. It had remained in that position come hail, come snow for as long as he could remember, and probably a lot longer. Through heavy rain, and strong winds. Through lightning, and heat wave, it hadn't moved. It had stood firm, seemingly rooted to the ground. *Just what was it doing there?* Ashby asked. Standing in the middle of a clearing like that. Just a solid door, and a solid frame, and that was that. Nothing more, just a simple door.

"Don't you ever go near it," his grandfather had said, pointing towards it, and shaking his head. David smiled as he remembered those words, "Don't you ever go near it." But it wasn't just the words, it was the way they had been said. He had sounded so dramatic, so forceful. His grandfather had died some years ago, but he could still hear those words as though they had been said just recently. He had to admit that his grandfather had certainly frightened him at the time, but he was always doing that. Telling ghost stories, or leaping out from behind a door, and crying out boo. He loved playing practical jokes on his grandson. But this was somehow different. This wasn't a joke. His entreaties were not said lightheartedly. He had sounded so serious, so definite, and there was a sense of urgency in his voice.

"There's danger lurking there," the grandfather had continued. "You mark my words, you heed my warning," wagging his finger for emphasis.

David laughed. "Danger" he murmured. "What danger?" he asked. It was just an old wooden paneled door, a very old wooden door, but a door nonetheless. In front of it was the forest. To each side was the forest. Behind it, there was nothing but the forest. So where was the danger? Was something going to suddenly leap out at him from behind the door? Was he going to be struck down by some invisible force? What harm could a door do, anyway?

His grandfather said nothing for a while, but continued to stare at the door. He then turned back to face Ashby. "Whatever you do, don't under-estimate what you see," he said quite slowly. "Things are not always what they seem" His voice would then drop to a whisper. "There are hidden forces we cannot control." He paused for a moment, and looked back at the door. "Just stay away from it, that's all. Stay away."

Ashby could hear the words clearly, and recalled the look on his grandfather's face. It was quite simply the look of fear. "It's a door, grand-dad," he had protested. "Just a door. There's nothing sinister about it. Nothing to be frightened of. Just an ordinary door. Don't worry so."

But was it just a door? Just an ordinary door?

"Is it?" replied his grandfather. "Are you sure there's nothing to worry about? Nothing to be afraid of? Are you absolutely certain that it is just a door, and nothing more?"

If it wasn't just a door, what was it? Ashby wondered. "Yes, Granddad, I'm absolutely sure," Ashby replied. "It's only a door. What else?" He started to laugh. He looked over at the door, then looked back at his grandfather. "Let me show you," he said as he started towards the door.

"Stop," his grandfather yelled. "Don't go near it."

Ashby stopped, and walked back to his grandfather, shaking his head, and laughing.

"It's no laughing matter," his grandfather continued. "You're wrong. It's not just a door. You just do what I say, you hear me. Just keep away from it."

Ashby wasn't ready to give up just yet. "Grand-dad, if it's not just a door, tell me, what is it?"

"You never mind about all of that," his grandfather replied dismissively. "You just keep away from it, that's all. Do as I say."

To add to his grandfather's entreaties, there were the many rumours that were being spread. There was talk of people going missing. Reports of strange lights coming from nearby, and unexplained noises emanating from the door. Ashby had never witnessed any of these lights, or heard any of these noises, and merely dismissed them as meaningless scaremongering. *They were just rumours, nothing more,* David would say. Where was the evidence? Where were the newspaper reports? Where were the witnesses, who had seen the lights, or heard the noises? There were none. What were the names of the missing people? And if they really were missing, were there any official searches undertaken? No, there weren't.

It was clear that the rumours were just that. Unsubstantiated rumours. The stories were nothing more than someone's imagination running away with them. They were just stories, local gossip, and the stuff of which legends are born. Stories with no real substance. Of course it was just a door, an ornate door maybe, but still just a door. But nonetheless, the rumours persisted, and the reports of strange happenings kept coming.

Ashby continued to stare at the door, his grandfather's words resonating loudly in his brain. Then he suddenly noticed something. Something very odd. Something quite strange. Something that he had never noticed before. All vegetation close to the door appeared to be dead. In fact everything within five metres of the door appeared to be lifeless, and there was a noticeable absence of wild life. Why had he not noticed this before? *Had it always been like that,* he wondered, and he just hadn't noticed? Hardly likely, he thought. Had something happened to cause this phenomenon? The weather perhaps. But why just that area by the door? Why not the entire clearing?

Ashby's knowledge of horticulture was non-existent, but he could see no obvious explanation. Beyond the five metres mark there was lush greenery, ferns and grasses as far as the eye could see, and wild flowers of every colour imaginable. And the wild life thrived. There were birds all around, and bees and butterflies in abundance. It was a mystery that Ashby could not resolve, just like the actual presence of the door itself.

Ashby wondered what others had thought when they saw the door. Standing there in the middle of a wood. What would they do, if anything? Had they also been warned to keep away? If so had they heeded the warnings, or had they simply ignored them? Had they playfully knocked on the door, and demanded it to open?

David wondered how it had actually managed to just stand there for so long, exposed to the weather as it was. He imagined that it looked just as it had when it was first erected. Sturdy, solid, mysterious.

David smiled. Yes it was mysterious and no mistake. And probably it could tell quite a story if it could talk. But what story would it tell? And just what building had it been part of? It was thought to be six or seven hundred years old. It never changed, and never seemed to suffer wear and tear. Some people said that it had been the main door to a school that had been destroyed in a fire. Others said that in its day it had probably been part of an old monastery, or perhaps a medieval castle, or maybe it had been a manor house. Now it was just a solitary door and frame. All traces of any kind of a building had long disappeared. In fact there were no records that indicated that any building of any kind had ever existed at the site. An Internet search had found nothing. Whether or not there had ever been a building was, however, irrelevant. What was important was the fact that the door was all that remained. Others had said that it had simply been erected by one of the local craftsmen, but still they never gave an explanation as to why, or how.

And just why should the building be gone, and yet the door remain. Mysterious yes, but it was just a door after all. "Don't ever go near it." Those words echoed in David's brain, over and over. *But why*, David wondered. If it was just a door what possible harm could it do? It could fall over, he guessed. That could give you quite a knock, he imagined. But it hadn't fallen in six hundred plus years had it, so it was hardly going to fall over now.

He sighed and shook his head. He looked around and smiled. The forest was deserted. There wasn't a sound. He shook his head once again as he slowly approached the door. The door was certainly solid, with thick black hinges holding it to the thick door frame. Old English oak, built to last. Then he saw the large ornamental door knocker. Black, solid, cast iron. He looked around once again. Still there was no sound. He started to laugh. "I wonder if anyone is in," he said to no one in particular. He reached for the knocker, and knocked as hard as he could. The sound resonated and echoed through the trees.

He knocked once again. "Open up," he called out mischievously. "Abracadabra, Open sesame." Then he started to laugh once again. How stupid, he thought. There was no one to answer the door, it was just the forest nothing more. There was no butler around, no housemaid. He glanced behind the door. There were no signs that a hall porter was going to come running to answer his calls. *"Please come in, sir,"* he said bowing, as though he were the porter.

Then Ashby abruptly stopped laughing as the door began to open. It was slowly at first, gradually getting quicker as the creaking grew louder. He quickly backed away. The door remained open as he slowly moved towards it. He peered through the opening. He could clearly see the forest on the other side. He backed up, and looked to the sides of the door. The forest was still there. He looked behind the door, sure enough there was the forest in all its glory.

"See grand-dad, told you so. Just a door, an ordinary door. So where is the danger?" he murmured as he stepped through. As he did so the door closed loudly behind him. The forest suddenly disappeared, and in front of him was a large hallway. Timber paneling adorned the walls. The floor was in stone flags. Opposite was a wide staircase. Hanging from the high ceiling was a chandelier. There was no sound, except for the ticking of a clock.

And the sound of his grandfather pleading with him, "Just stay away from it, that's all. Stay away."

Chapter Three
28th December 1890 – Lansdown School

Where on earth was he? Wherever it was he didn't belong there, and he needed to get away, and soon. He turned and reached for the door handle. He grabbed it and turned, but the door refused to open. He pulled at the handle, twisting it this way, and then that way, but the door remained stubbornly closed. He pushed and pulled, all to no avail. His grandfather's words *Keep away from it,* echoed through his brain. Over and over. Why, oh why, had he not listened? Why had he not heeded that warning? *He knew best, didn't he?* He tried the door once again. Still it remained tightly shut.

Suddenly he heard footsteps approaching. Someone was coming down the stairs. "Ah, Mr. Ashby, David … it is David I believe," said a voice. "So you've arrived. You're early."

Ashby looked up. "Er … yes, it is David," he stammered. "But how did you …."

"Welcome to Lansdown School. We've been expecting you," the voice continued. "The name's Lyons. Donald, or Donny as the boys call me. For my sins I'm the German teacher. I'm very glad to meet you." He held out his hand.

Just what was going on, Ashby wondered. He said nothing, and merely took hold of the outstretched hand.

"It's strange, I heard someone knocking, but that was all," said Lyons. He looked around. "And there's no one else here, so who let you in?"

Who indeed? Ashby wondered. "Oh, nobody actually let me in," Ashby replied quite truthfully. "The door was already open."

"Already open," repeated Lyons. "That cannot be."

Ashby heaved a sigh. "Well that's all I can tell you," he explained. "I knocked, and suddenly the door just opened."

Lyons was still puzzled. "Very strange," he said. He thought for a moment. "Perhaps it wasn't closed properly from last night." He shook his head. "But I locked it myself, and I'm sure that it was secure." He went to the door and pushed against it. "It seems firm enough now. I just don't understand it. That's never happened before."

"All I can say is to repeat that no one let me in," said Ashby. "But as you can see I am in."

Lyons smiled and nodded. "Yes, you are," he replied. He was still puzzled. He looked at the door once again, and then looked back at Ashby. "Your luggage arrived yesterday, and we have placed it in your room," Lyons continued. "But we weren't actually expecting you until tomorrow."

"My luggage has arrived?" Ashby murmured. "I never …."

"Yes, you travel quite light, I must say," replied Lyons. "Unless, of course, there's more to come."

Ashby shook his head. "No, I …. Er …. There's no more."

"So how was your journey?" Lyons asked. "I expect you came by one of those Horse drawn trams didn't you? I'm afraid they don't appeal to me."

Ashby said nothing for a moment. *Horse drawn trams,* he thought. What on earth was Lyons talking about? "Oh, yes …. my journey. Yes, it was quite a surprise," he answered.

"Surprise?" repeated Lyons. "In what way?"

"It wasn't exactly what I had expected," Ashby explained quite truthfully.

"Oh I see, I understand," replied Lyons. "I've never actually embarked on such a trip myself, but I have heard that they can be rather tiresome shall we say. Are you very near to Highgate West Hill?"

"Highgate West Hill?" Ashby repeated, more and more puzzled.

"Yes, isn't that where the trams start?" replied Lyons. "Not for me, though. I tend to use the steam railway myself. Anyway you're here now and that's all that matters isn't it?"

"Yes," replied Ashby. "I'm here now, as you say." *Although where here is*, he could only wonder. "You said that you were expecting me," said Ashby more and more perplexed.

"Certainly, we were expecting you," replied Lyons. "We got your letters. That last one said that you would be here tomorrow."

Ashby was becoming more and more perplexed. *How could it be that they were expecting him, when being here was a complete surprise to himself?* "But I've never written to the school," Ashby replied.

Now it was Lyons turn to look puzzled. "I don't understand," he said. "You applied for a position here. You are David Ashby, aged thirty-five, from Highgate? You do teach Art? Is that correct?"

Ashby had to admit that it was perfectly correct, every detail. "But how on earth do you know all of this?" he asked.

Lyons wasn't sure whether this was some kind of strange joke or not, but he wasn't amused. *Why is Ashby acting like this,* he wondered? "We've got all of your letters," he started to explain. "The first letter, the one when you were seeking employment, that's the one that gave the details I mentioned, the one you sent in October. And then we have your reply accepting our offer, just a couple of weeks ago."

"I never wrote any letters, I tell you," protested Ashby. "It's all some terrible mistake, I don't understand."

Clearly Ashby was stressed for some reason, the journey perhaps. Or maybe just the strangeness of new surroundings. Lyons smiled. "Of course you wrote the letters, there's no mistake," he said calmly. "I mean you wouldn't be here otherwise would you? You're just tired that's all."

Ashby shook his head. "I'm not tired," he replied. "October did you say? I wrote to you in October, and this is April."

"April?" repeated Lyons. "You're a little behind the times. This is December. And I think you must be more tired than you imagine."

"I repeat I never wrote any letters," insisted Ashby. "I have never heard of your school. I just don't understand any of this."

Lyons was feeling more and more, unsure of Ashby. *Perhaps he was feeling unwell. Or maybe now that he had arrived he was having second thoughts.* "Look we'll go and see Miss Taylor, she's the school secretary. She'll show you the letters." He looked at Ashby. Lyons had to admit that Ashby didn't look very well. "This way."

A few minutes later they arrived at Miss Taylor's office, and Ashby had been shown the letters.

"That is your signature isn't it?" asked Lyons, pointing at the bottom of the letter.

Ashby was more puzzled than ever. He had to admit that it was, but he still didn't understand what was happening. "But, I …."

Lyons then picked up another letter. "This is a copy of the letter that we sent to you." He showed it to Ashby. "It's the one where we offered you a position here." He then picked up another letter, and showed that to Ashby. "And this is your letter and look you actually say that you will be arriving here tomorrow, the 29th December, but of course you arrived a day early."

Ashby could not believe what he was hearing.

"So we know that you did write those letters, and that you were expected," said Lyons. "Do you agree?"

Ashby said nothing, but slowly nodded his head.

"Nonetheless, I can see that you are still puzzled," Lyons continued. "I know exactly why. You're wondering why the school is still open so close to the New Year."

That was certainly one question in Ashby's mind. But it wasn't his number one priority. "I did wonder about that," he replied.

"Well, it's quite simple really. Not every pupil has been fortunate enough to go home for the holiday, and this is a boarding school," Lyons started to explain. So several of them are required to stay here. We have eighty two boys with us, aged between eleven and sixteen." He paused for a moment. "But you knew that surely, wasn't it mentioned in our reply to your first letter? Perhaps it had just slipped your memory."

Ashby was still none the wiser regarding the situation he found himself in, *29th December, it didn't make any sense.* "Perhaps," he replied.

Lyons ignored how unconvinced Ashby sounded. "By the way did you know Wyndham?" he continued.

Ashby shook his head. "Wyndham?" he repeated.

"Wyndham is the, er, gentleman that you are replacing," Lyons explained.

Ashby shook his head. "No. No I don't think so," he replied.

"Oh, you would certainly remember him," said Lyons. "A thoroughly nasty individual I can tell you. So what misdemeanor did you commit for you to get sent here, to the Institution? Must have been really bad."

"I ... " Ashby began to stammer, and then paused *What had he done, apart from being stupid, and ignoring good advice. Could he just state his dilemma? Simply tell the whole story. I'm not sure how, or why, but I shouldn't be here. I come from another time. Lyons will be surprised, but he'll understand. He'll walk to the main door open it, I'll go out, and everything will be back to normal.*

"Are you alright my dear fellow?" asked Lyons. "You don't look too good. The journey I expect, after all you have come rather a long way haven't you?"

Well that was certainly true, Ashby thought. He had come from a long way, of that there was no doubt. "Oh, I'm fine thank you," he replied. "A bit tired perhaps."

"Right, you could do with a rest," replied Lyons. "I should have realised. My apologies for keeping you talking like this. Please forgive me. Perhaps a rest might do you some good. I'll take you up to your room."

* * *

They started up the stairs. Lyons suddenly stopped and pointed to one of the paintings that lined the staircase wall.

"There he is, bless him" Lyons announced. "Dr Roland Shutt, M.A. (Cantab.), P.H.D. (London), J.P., our illustrious Head Master."

The painting showed a rather stern looking man, wearing a winged collar, and a black gown. Ashby smiled. *The boys must have been terrified of him*, he thought.

"I'm afraid the Head Master isn't here right now, he had to go up to the City. School Board business I believe," Lyons said, as they continued up the staircase. "So it falls to me to give you a brief introduction. I promise that I'll keep it short." He took a deep breath. "We have five hundred and twenty-five pupils, aged between eleven and sixteen, registered at the school. As I told you most of them have gone home for the holiday, but we still have a hundred or so boys to look after. Normally there are twenty-two teachers, and of course matron. Couldn't forget her could we? She's the one really in charge and to be feared, not the Head."

"One hundred boys did you say?" repeated Ashby. "But I thought you had said that there were eighty-two."

Lyons smiled. "Yes, you are right, I did say eighty-two," he admitted. "But sometimes it just seems like one hundred. After a while, a very short while, you'll understand exactly what I mean."

Ashby smiled. "I look forward to discovering that myself," he replied. "All in good time, assuming that I'm still here." He looked at Lyons waiting to see his reaction. Lyons merely smiled. "So what about the staff?" Ashby continued, changing the subject. "You said there were twenty teachers."

"During term time there are twenty-two," Lyons corrected. "Of course most of the staff have gone home for the Christmas holidays. There's six of us, seven with you, who have decided to stay with the boys. Don't ask me why, although for my part I'm alone in this world. I have no relatives, my parents died a few years ago." He stopped and looked around. "So this is really home to me."

"What about the others?" Ashby asked. "Why have they decided to stay?"

"I've no idea," replied Lyons. "I've never asked them, nor would I. Maybe it's all to do with the extra payment we receive." He smiled, and nodded. "But what about you? Why have you decided to come at this time? Didn't you have other plans for the holiday?"

Ashby said nothing for a moment or two. *Yes, he certainly would have had far different plans, except Christmas had been several months away, so the question never arose.* "I have to say that I never actually gave it any thoughts," he replied quite truthfully. "It all happened so suddenly."

"To tell you the truth, we were actually surprised when you said that you were coming now, and not waiting for the New Year," said Lyons. "That's not to say we aren't pleased to see you. Quite the opposite in fact my dear sir. We are delighted you are here, you are more than welcome."

You were surprised, thought Ashby. He smiled. *But probably not as surprised as I was.* "Thank you," he replied simply.

They continued on their way upstairs. As they reached the top, Lyons spied a young boy running towards him. "Carter, we walk, not run," he called out. "Aren't you supposed to be at an English class with Mr. Sinton?"

"Yes sir," the boy replied nervously. "I'm late, sir."

"Well get along then," replied Lyons. "Don't keep Mr. Sinton waiting. You know he doesn't like that." He looked at Ashby and shook his head. "Boys," he said as he continued along the corridor. He suddenly stopped.

"Here we are," he announced. "This is your room. I'm further down the corridor." He opened the door, and beckoned Ashby to enter. "If you need anything just give a shout."

Once again David tried to speak, but could not find the words.

"I due to see Miss Taylor in a few minutes," Lyons announced. "Something to do with the pantomime we're taking the boys to see. So I must dash." With that Lyons hurriedly left.

Ashby shook his head. *What on earth was happening,* he wondered. Where was he? He slowly closed the door. Then he saw his luggage sitting in the middle of the room. He walked over to it, and tried to open it. It was locked. "Great" he murmured, as he reached inside his pocket for a handkerchief. Instead he withdrew a key. Perplexed more than ever he tried the key in the lock on the trunk. It opened. Inside were several books, and an assortment of clothing that he had never seen before. Clothing that seemed to be from another time. *Where was he?* More to the point, when was he?

It was then that he realised that Lyons would never have understood his dilemma, he did not understand it himself. His story was just too fantastic. Who would ever believe such a tale? At that instance he knew that the only way out was to escape but how?

* * *

Chapter Four
28th December 1890 –
New Surroundings

Ashby was becoming ever more despondent. His situation was looking hopeless. No one was going to believe him, and even if they did, would they be able to help him? It was becoming clear that his only chance of returning to normalcy was by going out the same way that he had come in. His only way out was through that door. That door that he had seen over so many years. That door that he had been warned about. *Keep away from it.* He frowned as he remembered what he had said. "It's a door, just an ordinary door." How wrong he had been.

It was not going to be easy. Indeed, so far he had made several attempts to open the door, but without success.

He looked around at his new surroundings. The room was small, and scantily furnished. A large oak wardrobe was located in one corner. Next to it was a large brass bedstead. By its side a bedside table. On the opposite wall was a roll top bureau. It was open. He walked over to it. He smiled as he noticed the blotter, and the ink well. Lying in a small tray was a selection of pens with nibs of various sizes. He started to laugh. He hadn't used a pen like that since .... *"Since when?"* he murmured. In fact he had never actually used such an item. *You don't need a pen to send an email,* he thought, *or to send a text.* Then he suddenly remembered something. His mobile phone, but where was it? *Somewhere back there,* he murmured, as he looked towards the door.

Then he saw something that horrified him. It was a calendar hanging on the wall. A calendar for the year 1890. The day was clearly marked with a red circle, 28th December. He stood up and walked towards it. "It really is December 28th" he murmured, hardly believing his eyes. "28th December, 1890," he repeated slowly. "It can't be," he said to no one. "It's not possible." He shook his head, and rubbed his eyes. *What on earth was going on,* he murmured. It was some kind of mad dream he was having.

Would he ever escape the madness? Would he ever return to his previous life, and return to 2021? He glanced back at the room, and started to cry. *Was this to be his fate for the remainder of his life?*

"Where am I?" he asked no one in particular. More to the point "When am I?" Once again he thought of the door. That solitary door in that clearing in the forest. It had been the springtime then, the fifth of April. It seemed a million miles away. It didn't make any sense. He shook his head. Clearly, somebody was having a very unfunny joke. Either a very bad joke, or a bad dream, or maybe both. It must have been a mistake. He closed his eyes. "When I open them again, it will prove I'm right, and that it was a mistake, and everything will be back to normal."

He counted to ten, and slowly opened his eyes. He looked around once again. There was no mistake. Indeed, if he had been completely honest he would have admitted that he never really believed that it was a mistake.

This was madness, he thought. Utter madness. It was indeed mad, but he knew that if he had said anything to anyone, it would be he that was judged mad. Indeed there were times when he had actually questioned his own sanity. After all there were those two letters that he had apparently sent. Then there was his luggage that had arrived, except, of course, the contents meant nothing to him. But then there was that key, the key that unlocked the trunk. The key that he had found in his jacket.

He had to get away from this place, and this time. Somehow, he needed to get back through that door, the main entrance door.

* * *

Ashby slowly opened his door, and peered out into the corridor. He saw no one. He heard no one. He stepped out of the room, quietly closing the door behind him, and made his way down the stairs. He then walked across the hall, and reached the entrance door. He looked around once again. There was no one around. He gripped the door handle and turned. The door remained closed. He tried again, pulling the handle towards him. It remained stubbornly closed. Disappointed he was about to try for a third time, when he heard someone coming down the stairs. It was Lyons.

Ashby looked around, desperately trying to find somewhere to hide. Then he saw a possibility. At the side of the staircase there was a small alcove. He ran to it. But he was too slow. "Ah there you are," said Lyons. "I've been looking all over, for you. So what are you doing?"

"Oh I was just looking around," replied Ashby.

At that moment there was a knock on the door. Lyons went to it and opened it. Ashby tried to peer though to the open countryside, but Lyons and another man blocked his view.

"Ah, welcome back Head Master," said Lyons, holding the door open. So how was your trip?"

The Head Master came into the hallway, and Lyons closed the door. "The same as ever. You know what these events are like," the Head Master replied. "Nothing but talk, talk, and more talk. Meaningless, with no substance. A complete waste of valuable …"

He suddenly noticed Ashby, still standing by the door. He looked at Lyons, and then looked back at Ashby. "I take it that you are our new Art teacher. Ashby isn't it?"

"Yes sir, I'm …." Ashby began, but the Head Master was no longer listening

The Head Master had turned back to Lyons, and continuing their conversation. "So Donny, what's been happening while I've been away," he asked. "How's our friend, Wyndham? Behaving himself I hope."

Lyons shook his head and smiled. "The same as ever, I'm afraid," he replied.

"Umm, come along and tell me all about it," the Head Master replied. The two men then walked away, in the direction of the Head Master's office.

The Head Master suddenly stopped and looked back at Ashby. "Ashby," he called out. "Perhaps you would be good enough to come and see me this evening, before supper." He paused for a moment. "Shall we say six o'clock?"

Without waiting for an answer, he turned back to Lyons. "Right, Donny, so start at the beginning, and tell me," he said. "I want to know everything."

* * *

At six o'clock precisely Ashby knocked on the Head Masters door.

"Come in," a voice called out.

Ashby opened the door, and entered the office.

"Ah Ashby, come in, come in," said the Head Master as Ashby peered around the door. "Do sit down." He looked up, as Ashby entered the room and took the chair that had been indicated.

"I just thought this would be a good opportunity to get to know each other," the Head Master said.

Ashby smiled and nodded.

"I was sorry to hear that you've had a few problems since you've arrived," the Head Master continued. "So what seems to be the problem?"

Ashby looked up but made no reply.

"Something about not writing those letters we had received," the head explained. "And apparently you were surprised that you had been expected. I cannot imagine why."

Ashby smiled. The Head Master's words came to mind. "I want to know everything." *Clearly Lyons had complied with the request, and told the Head Master everything,* he thought, but it was really no more than he had expected. In fact Ashby had to admit that in the circumstances it was probably a natural consequence, and quite understandable. "Oh that, that was nothing, Ashby replied. "Just my new surroundings I think. A little strange, that's all, oh, and being overtired."

"That's exactly what Donny had said," the Head Master replied. He wasn't entirely convinced however, but did not pursue the point. "Yes it must be a little strange for you," he replied. After all it must be a lot different to your last position." He paused, and looked at Ashby's letter. "A school in Highgate, I see." He paused once again, and continued reading the letter. "The Sir Roger Cholmeley's School, in fact," he continued. "Very impressive. An excellent school by all accounts. Nonetheless, I'm sure that you will agree that there is a vast difference between Highgate, and here in Hampstead. But I'm sure that you will get used to us in no time at all." He started to smile. "Of course that applies both ways you know."

Ashby looked puzzled.

The Head Master started to laugh. "After all, we have to get used to you, don't we?"

Ashby smiled, and nodded. "Yes sir, that's very true." *But it's not the people that's the problem,* he thought. *It's the time period.* "I'm sure that it will all come right in the end," he said.

The Head Master wasn't entirely sure what was meant by that last remark, but he let it go. "I understand that you came here on one of those horse drawn trams, is that right?" the Head Master continued. "What did you think of them?"

Good question, thought Ashby. *What did I think, considering I've never been on a tram, horse drawn, or otherwise, in my entire life.* "Well, I have to say …. That I would not recommend them."

Doctor Shutt started to laugh. "My sentiments exactly," he replied. "Just what I thought when I took my first, and I have to say, my very last, trip on one."

The Head Master continued reading the paper that was lying in front of him. "Incidentally, I thought you told Donny that all of your luggage had arrived?" He looked up at Ashby.

Ashby nodded. "Yes, that's what I said," he replied. "I think that's correct. I'm sure that I'm not expecting anything …."

"Well, that small valise arrived this afternoon." The Head Master pointed to the corner. "It's yours I believe. You can take it with you when we are finished." He paused for a moment. "Now, I don't suppose that you know very much about us do you? You probably have several questions you would like to ask."

Ashby smiled, *if you really want the truth, I don't know anything about you at all.* "That's true, sir," he replied. "I would be interested to know more."

The Head Master smiled. He was delighted. He enjoyed talking about his beloved school more than any other subject. "Now, I know that Donny has told you a few things, so I might be repeating certain details, but please bear with me."

Ashby nodded.

"Donny, did mention that you were wondering about the date being within the holiday period," the Head Master began. "He also pointed out that you were wondering why the school was still open"

"That's correct, sir," replied Ashby. "My last school would close at least one week before Christmas, and re-open on the 6th or 7th in the New Year."

"Yes I understand," replied the Head Master. "And in a, shall we say, normal school that would be considered quite reasonable." He smiled. "Here things are a little different. Lansdown Industrial School was founded in 1819, by Henry Lansdown. It moved to its present site twenty-five years later. Mr Lansdown had made his money as a brewer. His original plans for the school was to give opportunity to the poor, and in particular he had in mind orphan children, or children whose parents were …. Er …. Residing in the Workhouse, or worse still, in one of Her Majesty's prisons."

"So the school is just eighty years old," Ashby said. "Are those aims still in force?"

"They are indeed, however, time has resulted in some changes," the Head Master replied. "The school was taken over by the County Council in 1869, and we were obliged to allow other boys to come to us. But of course we still have a large number of those fitting the original plan." He paused for a moment and looked at Ashby. "And now we come to the answer to your original concerns. Currently the Lansdown School has five hundred and twenty five students, ranging from eleven years old up to fifteen, registered with us. Due to circumstances, many of the poorer pupils have no one to go to over the holiday period. So we keep them here."

"How about the teachers?" asked Ashby.

"Ah, the teachers, why are they still here? A good question," said the Head Master. "We have a staff of twenty-two teachers, er twenty three now that you are here. But at the present time there are only seven teachers and myself, to look after 82 children. Of course I should add Mrs Taylor, the school secretary and Miss Bradley, the matron. Where would we be without our nurse?" He smiled. "They stay simply as an act of loyalty to the school. In other words, they volunteer, they request permission to stay."

"I see," replied Ashby. "I imagine you provide a wide range of subjects."

"Ah yes, we do," replied the Head Master. "The school caters for a wide variety of subjects including arithmetic, reading and writing, together with geography, history, French, in fact we have two French masters, so we are quite fortunate in that respect, science, and now of course, art."

The Head Master paused for a moment. He glanced at the clock on the wall. He then turned back to face Ashby. "Now you have some idea of our background, perhaps you've changed your mind about joining us?"

Ashby wondered if this was the opportunity he had been looking for. A possible chance to escape. *What would happen if I said, yes, I've changed my mind? Would they open that door, and let me walk through, and if that happened would I be returned to my time, and back to that forest clearing?* Equally important, what would happen if he actually agreed to stay? *Would that mean he would never be able to leave?* So many questions. How should he answer? "Well, er …."

"As I thought, good man," the Head Master interrupted. Ashby's questions were not to be answered. His chance, whatever it was, had gone. "I just knew you would decide to stay," the Head Master continued, a huge smile on his face. "And no more talk about not belonging, right? When I first saw your letter of application, I knew right away. In fact I said so to Miss Taylor, and Mr. Lyons. You were right for the school. Firm, but fair. That's what I say. The boys need discipline. The boys need guidance, but we need to be firm but fair. That is our way. The Christian way. Don't you agree?"

Ashby was about to make a reply, when the Head Master began once again. "I've been looking through your qualifications. Very impressive. Very impressive indeed."

"Thank you, sir," said Ashby.

"But I have to admit that I am slightly puzzled," the Head Master continued.

You and I both, thought Ashby. *Although I'm a lot more than just slightly puzzled.* "Puzzled, sir," he repeated. "What is the problem?"

"Not a problem as such," explained the Head Master. "No, just curious. He started to tap the desk. Then he stopped. "I was just wondering why such a well-qualified person, as yourself, would end up at our school. Surely one of the Universities would have been more suitable."

Ashby wasn't really sure how to answer the point. After all he wasn't actually there by choice. "I have to admit that I have given a lot of thought as to where I wanted to teach," he paused reflecting on the fact that it was perfectly true, he had spent much time considering which direction to take. "All that I can say, is that something brought me here. I don't exactly know what that something was, but er ....here I am."

"Yes, as you say, here you are," the Head Master agreed. "And very pleased we are to have you. I hope that you will be happy here."

"Thank you, Head Master," said Ashby, knowing full well how much he longed to leave the place. He stood up.

"Incidentally, because it is so close to the New Year, I think we'll leave the Art lessons until January," the Head Master continued. "Unless you have other ideas."

"Oh no, no other ideas," said Ashby. "It will give me a chance to find my way around." *Or find a way out of here,* he thought.

"Off you go, then," the Head Master said. "And don't forget to take that with you." He pointed to the valise.

* * *

Ashby picked up the case and returned to his room. For some minutes he simply stared at it, lying on the floor. He was almost afraid to open it. Afraid of what it contained. Maybe further evidence to show he really did belong in this place, and this time. He picked it up and placed it on the bed. He then loosened the leather strap that was around the valise. He took a deep breath, and opened the case. Inside was a small photograph in a silver frame. He picked it up and looked at it. He gasped, and dropped the frame to the floor. The frame burst open and the glass shattered.

His worst fears had been realised. The photograph showed David Ashby, as a young man. It was a studio portrait, and was apparently taken in Highgate, on the 12th September 1875.

* * *

Mr David Ashby
12 September 1875

174 Highgate Hill
LONDON

Chapter Five
29th December 1890 –
A Kind Of Nightmare

The following morning Ashby was awake early. As usual, he hadn't slept well. Too much on his mind. Too much that he didn't understand.

So his second day in this strange place, and time, had begun. Why had he not listened to his grandfather, and heeded his words? What had ever possessed him to be so foolish, so arrogant? He thought for a moment or two. "Yes," he murmured. "It had been arrogance on my part. I knew better, or so I thought."

He had considered his grandfather to be the stupid one, and his words were judged to be merely the ramblings of an old man. Just ramblings, nothing more. Ashby smiled. But his grandfather had been right hadn't he? His grandfather had been one hundred percent right. And it was he, Ashby, who had been the stupid one, and now he was paying the price for his error. A high price. What was he to do? How could he get away, back to normality?

So what does today have in store for me? He wondered. "I might as well get up," he murmured. *There was no point just lying there.* Lying there, just thinking, and getting more and more depressed. More and more stressed. As though things weren't bad enough, with the luggage, the key, now there was that photograph.

Where on earth had it come from, he wondered. But on closer inspection it became apparent that there was no mystery. The answer was there, right in front of him, on the photograph itself. A photographic studio somewhere in Highgate had taken it. And somebody had written the date, across the photograph. 12th September 1875. But who had written it?

He looked closer at the writing. It had clearly been written in a hurry, with very little consideration for neatness. There was no mystery. The identity of the writer was all too clear.

"That's my handwriting, I can't believe it," Ashby murmured. "It just can't be true. I've never seen that photograph before, so how could I ...."

Clearly it had been set up in some way. Impressive certainly, but who was doing this, and why? *What was happening,* he wondered? It was a kind of nightmare he was living in, a very bad dream. If he could just wake up the nightmare would come to an end, and things would be back to reality, back to normal. He would be back in that clearing in the forest, and about to get home before the rain started.

But he was already awake, and the nightmare hadn't come to end. He knew all too well, that it wasn't a dream. It was reality, at least a kind of reality. But a reality he never understood. A reality that was alien to him. He needed to escape, to get out of this madness that he was living in.

* * *

He slowly came down the stairs. The hallway was deserted. There was no sound, except for the ticking of the clock. He looked around. There was no one about. He walked over to the door. He placed his hand on the panelling. His escape, his salvation, his own sanity, lay beyond that door. Just on the other side was the freedom from the madness that he desperately sought. It must open, he murmured over and over. He placed his hand on the handle, turned it, and pulled hard. The door refused to open. Ashby tried again, still it would not open. He tried a third time. Still there was no movement. It was hopeless. In his desperation there came thoughts of actually breaking the door down.

* * *

He was about to walk away when he heard someone approaching on the outside. The sound came ever closer, then there was a knock on the door. Ashby looked around to see if anyone was going to answer it. No one came. *It was a golden opportunity, maybe,* he thought. He reached for the handle once again, and turned. The door opened wide. "Freedom at last," he murmured.

However, Ashby's route to freedom was being blocked. A rotund man, with a ruddy face was standing between him and the end to his nightmare.

The man smiled. "Ah, its Mr. Ashby isn't it?" he said. "They told me you'd be coming about now. I'm right pleased to meet you, sir. The old school could certainly use another teacher, and no mistake."

Ashby wasn't listening. He was looking out beyond the man, looking for the forest clearing where he had been, just a few days ago. There was no clearing, and no signs of a forest. Instead there was a horse drawn milk cart, standing in a gravelled driveway. Beyond was nothing but the school wall.

"Hoping I'm not speaking out of turn, sir," Daniel continued. "But that Mr. Wyndham won't be missed, not by a long way, I can tell you."

"Mr. Wyndham?" Ashby repeated. "I don't know …."

"The teacher whose place you are taking," explained Daniel. "Did nobody tell you? I thought that they would have mentioned it."

"No, no one has said anything," replied Ashby, forgetting the brief remark made by Lyons. "At least not yet."

"Maybe, I shouldn't be saying anything," Daniel said. "I'm always putting my foot in it. I speaks too much, that's what my wife says, and I expects …."

Ashby shook his head. "No, no, you shouldn't worry like that," he replied. "No harm done. Least said soonest mended as they say."

Daniel had no idea what Ashby was saying. "So you won't be saying anything then?" Daniel replied. "I wouldn't want Mr. Lyons to be knowing what I said. He's a good man, don't get me wrong, but he can be a bit …. Well you know what I'm saying. He don't stand for any gossip, so to speak."

Ashby shook his head once again. "Not a word, so don't worry," he said, touching Daniel's arm. "He won't hear anything from me."

There was an awkward silence for a few moments. It was broken by Daniel. "You're up and about nice and early, young sir," the man continued, changing the subject. "Mind you, I'm an early riser myself. Got to be, you understand, things to do," He looked back at the cart. "I need to be up and out delivering the milk you see. Four o'clock is my time, and not a minute later. That's the way of it. Been that way for twenty odd years or more."

He looked at Ashby and smiled. Ashby said nothing. "Right, I must get on. I'll just leave this down in the hall for you then." He placed a milk churn in the hallway, together with a small package. "Them's are sausages," he explained. "They're for Mr. Eaton".

Ashby moved back, out of the way. Then he suddenly stopped and looked out on to the gravelled driveway, and at the horse and cart. "Just a minute Mr. er ...." He started to say, a vague idea forming in his head.

"Daniel'll do right enough, sir."

"I just thought that I'd like to see your horse", said Ashby. "If that was alright with you."

Daniel turned and looked at the horse. "Ah that's Jenny, sir," Daniel replied. "She's a fine old horse, none better."

"Could I go and see her?" Ashby asked.

"Certainly you can, sir," replied Daniel. "It'll be my pleasure."

Ashby's plan, although vague, was about to be blocked before it even got started.

"I say, I wouldn't go out there if I were you," a voice called out. "I think you best stay in. It looks like it is going to rain."

Instinctively, Ashby turned and reluctantly stepped back into the hallway."

"Never mind, sir. Maybe next time," said Daniel. "I'll get the door for you, sir, you don't trouble yourself." Daniel pulled the door closed.

Ashby moved forward and reached for the door before it closed completely, but it was not to be. He then heard the footsteps gradually fading. And then, a moment of two later came the sound of the cart moving away. He reached for the door handle once again. Turned it. As he had come to expect, the door remained firmly shut.

Ashby was more puzzled than ever. That man, Daniel, seemed to know him, or at the very least knew of him. More than that, he actually expected to see Ashby. The madness continued.

"Hello," cried a voice from behind Ashby. "It's Ashby, isn't it? I'm Eaton. Robert Howard Eaton. Rob to my friends." He held out his hand. "You're up and about bright and early aren't you?"

Ashby reached forward. "Yes, I'm Ashby, David. Pleased to meet you," he replied, although by actually acknowledging Eaton, and shaking his hand, he was only adding to the madness that was going on around him. "Oh yes," Ashby continued. "I couldn't sleep, so I got up. No point in just lying there."

Eaton nodded. "Strange bed I guess, you'll get used to it," he replied. "Incidentally, I'm the French teacher. Well, that is I'm one of them. We also have Alec. Alec Aldridge, he's several years my senior, but a real gentleman." He paused waiting for a response from Ashby. There was none. "Hmm, you teach Art I understand?"

Ashby confirmed that he was indeed the Art teacher.

"Interesting," Eaton replied. "I wonder what you think of these new artists, these er, Impressionists I think they are called?"

"Yes, that's the correct term," agreed Ashby. "I actually like that style very much."

"I'm not entirely sure, myself. All looks a bit blurred to me, out of focus if you like," said Eaton. "Although, I have to admit that I think Renoir is quite good. I really liked that one he did three or four years ago. What was it called?" He paused for a moment. "Ah I remember, it was Les Parapluies. Sorry, that's French for The Umbrellas. Do you know it?"

Ashby nodded. "Oh yes, I know it, but surely it was painted a lot longer than four years ago."

"Really? You might be right, after all you are the Art teacher, so you should know," admitted Eaton. "Although I was sure it was painted in 1886."

"That's right it …." Ashby suddenly realised his mistake.

Eaton suddenly noticed the milk churn, and the package, lying in the hallway. "I see that old Daniel has been round. Cheerful as ever I suppose. Delivered the milk, and the sausages. Good show. I better get them over to the kitchen," he said. "I expect I'll see you in the Common Room later."

Ashby watched him as he went down the corridor. Then he looked back at the door, considering whether he should give it another try. He heaved a sigh. He had been unsuccessful so many times. He walked over to the door, and took hold of the handle. He took a deep breath, and was about to try one more time, when he sensed someone standing behind him.

* * *

Chapter Six
29th December 1890 –
The Common Room

"Ashby! What are you up to," a voice called. "It's me, Lyons. I went to your room, but of course you weren't there. Then I thought I heard old Daniel."

Ashby turned and nodded. "You did," he replied. "He brought some milk, and …. And sausages. Someone, Eaton I think he said his name was. Yes, Mr. Eaton took them to the kitchen. I was just about to go back to my room."

"Ah, glad I caught you then," said Lyons. "I thought you might like to see the grounds Then I want to introduce you to some of the others. I'll take you along to the Common Room"

Outside, Ashby thought. Maybe a chance to escape this madness. A slim one maybe, but a chance nonetheless, and a chance he had to take. "Be right with you," he replied.

"Incidentally do you play Rugger?" Lyons asked.

Ashby was intrigued. "No I'm afraid not," he replied.

"Pity," said Lyons. "What about Cricket?"

Ashby smiled. "When I was younger, yes I played a bit, but not so much now," he replied. "Why do you ask?"

"The thing is we really need a Sports Master, and, well I just thought that maybe … well not to worry. See you back here, in what? Ten minutes?"

* * *

Ten minutes later Ashby was waiting by the front door. There was no sign of Lyons. Ashby was disappointed. His possible chance of escape was fading fast.

"There you are," called Lyons as he came into the hallway. "I've been waiting at the back door. Then I suddenly realised that you would be here. My fault I should have made it clear. Sorry."

"The back door?" repeated Ashby, clearly disappointed.

"Yes, you see the back door leads straight on to the tennis courts and the playground," Lyons explained. "Come along, this way."

Ashby followed. *So it wasn't the front door,* he thought. *But it was still outside, and there was still a chance of getting away.*

"Here we are," said Lyons as they reached the back door. He opened the double doors wide. "There it is. What do you think?" He pointed to a large playground marked out for various games. Over in the far corner were two tennis courts.

Ashby looked and tried to smile. There was no signs of the forest area that he had been expecting to see. Nothing familiar. "Very nice," he mumbled.

"Very nice, did you say?" replied Lyons, sounding disappointed. "Very nice. Is that all you can say? Why there's not a free school anywhere in England with such an area, or tennis courts. Oh certainly public schools like Harrow or Eton would have them but not a school like ours."

"No, of course not," Ashby quickly replied. "Absolutely true, I'm very impressed. Do many of the boys play tennis?"

Lyons smiled, beginning to feel much better. "Oh yes we have one or two who are quite good," he replied. "I'll arrange a match so that you can judge for yourself." He started to close the doors. "In the meantime I think that we'll go along to the Common Room and I'll introduce you to the others." He smiled. "You'll like that I'm sure."

Ashby wasn't looking forward to it, but clearly he had no choice. "Right, lead on, I'm right behind you."

* * *

Ashby was immediately set upon, as he entered the Common Room. "So you're Ashby," said a voice angrily. "My replacement." The voice was slurred, as though the person had been drinking. "I'm Wyndham, in case you hadn't realised."

"Leave it alone, Wyndham," a voice called out.

"You've been drinking again, Wyndham," cried another.

Ashby looked up.

"Yes, I'm talking to you," Wyndham continued. "I suppose you're pleased with yourself aren't you? Don't worry about me whatever you do."

"I'm sorry, I ..." stammered Ashby.

"You're sorry," repeated Wyndham, as he turned to face the others. "Do you hear that, everybody. He's sorry. Everybody's sorry." Wyndham shook his head and looked back at Ashby. "You're not one bit sorry, you're not sorry at all. Why should you be sorry? You don't know me, but you've just taken my position here at the school that's all. No you're not sorry, you're pleased."

"Wyndham, let it go," Lyons out. "Why are you still here anyway? Shouldn't you be gone by now."

"There speaks the great, Mr. Lyons. Donny to his friends, that's why I call him Mr. Lyons," Wyndham replied. "Don't worry, I won't stay any longer than I have to." With that Wyndham hurried form the room.

"Thank goodness he has gone," said Lyons. Heaving a sigh. "I'm sorry about that, Ashby. I should have warned you. Anyway, let me introduce you to everyone. Sitting in the far corner is Robert Eaton, but you've already met him. Next to him is Walter Spooner, Wally to his friends," Lyons commenced. "Our geography master. Next we have the other French master, remember I told you, Alec Aldridge."

"Hello, I'm James Shivas," a voice said coming over and offering a hand to Ashby. "I'm the English teacher, one of them."

Ashby reached forward and took hold of the outstretched hand.

"Mr. Shivas has been here at Lansdown for over twenty years," explained Lyons.

"Actually, it's nearer thirty," Shivas corrected. "Welcome, Mr. Ashby, and I hope you have a happy time here." Ashby smiled. *Oh, I'm having a wonderful time,* he thought.

Someone sitting a short distance away, raised his hand. "Let me introduce myself," a voice announced. "I am Dr. Lambert, I am from Belgium. I have been in this country for almost thirty-five years, and I am the Science teacher."

"He teaches the boys how to make explosives," explained Lyons. "So that they can destroy their classroom."

"Ah, yes, but we don't stop there," said Lambert. "Oh no, we wish to destroy the entire school, and we will one day." He nodded and smiled.

"Well there we are then," said Lyons. "It seems that while most of us are trying to instil good Christian values into our pupils, the good doctor is planning on total destruction."

Ashby started to laugh. He stopped abruptly as the door opened and the Head Master walked in. A hush fell over the room. "Is anyone going to explain what was so amusing?" he asked. "You, Mr. Ashby, perhaps." Ashby remained silent. "Then maybe you Mr. Lyons. Please enlighten me."

"Oh, it was nothing really, sir," Lyons replied. "I was just explaining to Ashby here about the pantomime we have planned for this evening."

"Oh, I see, but please do go on," said the Head Master. "I fail to see anything humourous about Cinderella."

"Well you see, sir, it's quite simple," Lyons replied. "Ashby remembers it from his childhood, and he always found the ugly sisters to be amusing."

The Head Master nodded, still far from being amused. "Possibly," he replied. He looked at Ashby. "So how are you getting along?" He looked over at Lyons. "I understand that Mr. Lyons has been showing you around. Is that right?"

"Oh yes, sir, he has been looking after me," replied Ashby. "The school is very impressive I must say. I can't wait until I can start teaching." He suddenly realised what he had said. He was beginning to encompass what was happening to him. Joining in with conversations, as though it were the most natural thing. More and more he seemed to be accepting his situation. Accepting it as normal, and no longer fantasy.

"That's good to hear," said the Head Master. "I like my colleagues to be enthusiastic. But I'm afraid you must curb your enthusiasm, at least for the time being. Until the new year, and then let the art lessons begin." He looked around the Common Room. There was spontaneous applause from the others. "There you are," he continued. "In the meantime, I trust that you will enjoy the pantomime later today, at two thirty I believe." He quickly glanced around the room, and hurried out.

The Head Master was right, thought Ashby. He really must curb his enthusiasm. Enthusiasm for the school, which in the reality of his own time, 2021, no longer existed.

For the teachers, decent people certainly, but all of them long since dead. *Pantomime,* thought Ashby. The very last thing he needed was additional fantasy. His life was one long pantomime at present.

However, perhaps it could be another opportunity to escape.

"Where do we go for the pantomime? He asked.

"Oh, not far," replied Lyons. "Not far at all."

* * *

Later that afternoon Lyons, Shivas, and Ashby, together with thirty of the older boys, were taken to a small theatre in the local village to see a performance of Cinderella. It was an amateur production, and although the boys seemed to enjoy it, Ashby had spent most of the time looking for an opportunity to get away.

Two hours later the school party returned to the school. Clearly the pupils had enjoyed it, but Ashby had found the whole event extremely boring, and had offered no chance of escape. He returned to his room more and more depressed.

How could he ever get away from the place, when he didn't really understand how he had got there in the first place?

* * *

Chapter Seven
30th December 1890 –
Thoughts of Escape

Ashby's mind was in turmoil. He thought of the recent events over and over. It made no sense. Everyone, including old Daniel, seemed to know all about him. His arrival had not been a surprise to anyone, except that he was a day early. He had been expected by everyone. His luggage had arrived, although where from he had no idea. *And who had sent it,* he wondered. Certainly he hadn't. Or had he? He was beginning to suspect his own mind. Everyone had accepted him, as though it were the most natural thing in the world. Were they right, and he the only one who was wrong? Could it be that his thoughts were the fantasy. That the here and now, December 1890, was the reality?

The letters he had been shown, the ones that he had allegedly written, looked genuine enough, and the signature was certainly his. Of that there was no doubt. To all the world he had signed documents that he would swear in Court, that he had never seen in his life. And yet the evidence was there for all to see. Crystal clear, and over whelming. And then there was that photograph. A photograph that he had never seen before. Or had he seen it, but his mind was blocking it for some unknown reason?

"I must get away," he murmured as thoughts of escape enveloped his mind. "But how?" There was always that question. How? Was it actually possible? Perhaps somewhere there was an answer to that question. Perhaps somewhere there was a possible way out. An escape route. All he had to do was find it. But if he did find a way, an escape, where would it lead him?

Certainly the key to everything was that door. Ashby had tried the door and it had failed to open, except once. The time that Daniel had been outside, he had managed to open the door easily. So why had it not opened on those other occasions. Other people seemed to have no problem. *So why should they be successful, and yet I fail?* He wondered.

* * *

Ashby had made his way to the hallway. *There must be a way to open that door,* he murmured. *Some special way of holding the handle, maybe. Or how the handle was turned.* And yet he knew that it was a simple handle, and others managed to operate it without a problem. Then he suddenly realised that it wasn't just the door that was a problem. It was what existed beyond the door. When Lyons had opened the door outside was a gravelled driveway, and a high brick wall. When Ashby had opened the door for Daniel, it was the same. There was no sign of the clearing in the forest that he knew.

He looked at the door, and shook his head in despair. His situation was looking hopeless. He walked closer to the door, his hands outstretched. He would try the handle once more. If that didn't work, he would find some way of breaking the door down.

As he approached the door a voice called out. "Hey Ashby." It was Lyons, he was with a group of boys. "Ashby," he called once again.

Ashby looked up and waved.

"Care to join us," Lyons continued. "I'm the Games master today, we take it in turns you know. We are just on our way out, for some physical exercises. I just thought you might like to join in. You'll need to know what to do anyway, when you turn comes."

"My turn?" repeated Ashby.

"Certainly, didn't you hear what I said?" Lyons replied. "We all take turns. Well at least the fit ones do, so poor old Aldridge, and Shivas they aren't included. They miss out on that pleasure. Anyway are you coming?"

Ashby looked at Lyons for a few moments. He would have preferred staying where he was, and examining that door closely, and trying it once again, but Lyons wasn't about to give up.

"Come on and join us," coaxed Lyons. "Better than hanging around inside."

Ashby had to admit that although it wasn't exactly the outside that he had in mind, at least it was outside, and maybe, just maybe, it would present an opportunity to get away. "Yes, I'm coming," he replied as he hurried over to join Lyons.

Arriving at the back door, Ashby looked out. The playground was surrounded by a high brick wall. Just the other side of that wall was the freedom he was seeking, or at least that was his hope.

"It's a bit cold though isn't it," Ashby announced, wrapping his arms around his body. He looked up at the sky. "It looks like we might have some snow."

Lyons smiled. "Oh maybe, but in the meantime a bit of exercise won't do any harm," he replied. "Besides a few minutes, and you'll feel as warm as toast.

"If you say so," replied Ashby, as he came alongside Lyons.

"I'm glad you're here," said Lyons "I need to go inside for a moment. Could you take over?"

The last thing on Ashby's mind was a bit of exercise. Nonetheless, he thought there could be a possible opportunity to get away. "You planned this didn't you?"

Lyons shrugged his shoulders. "The thought never crossed my mind."

"Oh, certainly, go on," Ashby replied. "Take as long as you need. I'll get the boys running around the perimeter wall."

"Good idea. I won't be too long," said Lyons, as he hurried back inside the building.

Ashby watched him go, and then turned towards the boys. "Hello boys, I'm Mr. Ashby," he announced.

"We know who you are, sir," replied one of the boys.

"You're our new Art teacher," added another. "We've been expecting you."

Even they were expecting me, Ashby thought. *But how did they know, when I didn't know myself?* It made no sense. He looked at the boys and heaved a sigh. "Right, boys, shall we have a run then?" he said, more determined than ever to get away.

The boys sounded less than enthusiastic. "Right off we go then," Ashby coaxed. "Hurry now. Once round, and then into the school for lemonade and cakes." That was all the encouragement the boys needed. They hurried away, closely followed by Ashby.

A short distance along the wall Ashby noticed a wrought iron gate. It was locked with a padlock and chain. The lock and chain was substantially rusted, and clearly the gate had not been opened for some time. He stopped and looked through the bars. There was no sign of a forest, or of the clearing where he had been walking just a few days before. In fact there was nothing that he recognised.

He continued to stare at the gate, and wondered if he could climb over it. *It certainly looked easy enough, but what was on the other side,* he wondered. *Where was he exactly? Was the clearing nearby?* Nothing seemed familiar. He looked through the bars once again. A short distance away he could see what he thought was a narrow pathway. *Where did it lead,* he wondered?

"How are they treating you, Ashby?" a voice cried out. Lyons had returned. "I hope they have been behaving themselves."

"Oh, yes they were fine," said Ashby. "No trouble at all, but I did promise them cakes, hope that was alright."

Lyons smiled. "They'll thank you for ever," he replied. "You'll be their friend for life.

Ashby looked back at the gate. "There's a pathway out there. Where does it lead?"

Lyons walked up to the gate. "Oh that one, that leads to St. Andrews," he replied. "That's the parish church of Heybridge, the local village."

"How far is that?" Ashby asked.

"Oh, about five or six miles," Lyons replied. "Why do you ask?"

"Oh no reason, just curious," replied Ashby, as he turned away from the gate. "I like to know about the local area that's all."

The village of Heybridge meant absolutely nothing to him. It wasn't familiar at all. He looked back towards the gate, and shook his head. He realised that if he did succeed in climbing the gate, and got to the village, he would only be exchanging one place for another. He would still be imprisoned in the same madness. *So I escape from here, but where will it get me, I still need to get back, back to my home.* Then the truth finally struck him.

"It's not just a place I want to escape from, it is also a time." He also knew that he could only really escape by going back through the door, the main entrance in the hallway. Nothing else mattered.

* * *

Chapter Eight
31st December 1890 –
The Morning

Once again Ashby had had a sleepless night. He was becoming more and more anxious about his situation. As time went on he became more and more resigned that he might never escape. He may have to spend the rest of his life in the new situation he was in.

He needed to speak to someone, but who? More importantly, would they believe him? There were times when he hardly believed it himself. Would they understand what he was saying, or would he merely be judged as being mad? The ranting of a lunatic. But what could he do. If he told them would they just tell everyone else? Or would they help him? More to the point, would they be able to help him?

There seemed no way out, except perhaps through that main door. But try as he might he could not open it. But if someone else opened it, and he then pushed his way past, and out of the building, then, maybe, he would get away, back to his own time and place. *But who was that someone else going to be,* he wondered?

* * *

"Ah Ashby, bright and early again." Lyons came down the stairs, and over to where Ashby was standing. "You know, I've never known anyone quite so keen to be up and about their business, as you are."

"Well I …." Ashby started to explain.

"So what are you planning today?" Lyons asked. "After all its New Year's Eve, the last day of the year," he rambled on.

"Tomorrow is a new day, a new year. So what are you looking forward to, for 1891?"

Ashby wasn't too concerned about the next day, or indeed the New Year. 1891 meant nothing to him, after all his year was 2021, one hundred and thirty-one years difference.

"Are you okay?" asked Lyons. "Another bad night?"

Ashby made no reply

"You should ask Matron for some sleeping pills," suggested Lyons. "They should help you get some rest. She'll have you right in no time."

"It's nothing to do with the lack of sleep," replied Ashby.

"You should still see Matron, she's very good with all kinds of maladies, and she knows the remedies required," suggested Lyons. "She/s very fond of those alternate remedies, you know, things like herb tea, and ...."

"Donny," Ashby stammered. "I need to talk to someone. Can you spare some time?"

Lyons was surprised at the urgency of Ashby's voice. "Oh my dear sir, of course I can. What seems to be the trouble, old man? Is it the boys? They can be difficult, I know, but they aren't that bad once you get used to them."

Ashby shook his head. "It's not the boys," he replied.

"How about the Head Master?" Lyons suggested. "Has he been laying down the heavy hand? You shouldn't worry about him, his bark is a lot worse than his bite. You'll get used to him in no time at all."

"Oh no, it's nothing like that," Ashby replied. "I've known Head Masters like him all over, and many of them a hundred times worse."

"Then it's got to be Wyndham," suggested Lyons. "He was laying it on a bit thick the other day I grant you. But you shouldn't take any notice of him, he'll be gone soon anyway."

"It's not Wyndham," said Ashby.

Lyons was puzzled. "Not Wyndham, not the boys. What then? One of the other teachers?"

"No it's nothing like that," interrupted Ashby. "The teachers are fine. It's just I don't belong here. Simple as that."

"Oh I see," replied Lyons. "Think you're not good enough, eh. Well I felt that way when I first arrived at Lansdown. Quite a reputation to live up to, it can be quite daunting. You shouldn't worry about that. After all, it's early days yet, you'll fit in right enough, I can ...."

"No," cried Ashby forcibly. "I don't fit in, simple as that. I don't understand any of this, but I shouldn't be here. I don't understand how I even got here."

"But the letters," said Lyons. "You applied for a position, and you …."

"I never wrote any letters," Ashby insisted. "Whoever wrote them I don't know, but it wasn't me."

Lyons heaved a sigh. "Oh no we're not going through that again are we?"

"It's true Donny, I never wrote those letters," said Ashby much calmer. "I have to tell someone. I'm sorry Donald, but I must leave, I have to get away, but I can't do that alone. My only escape is through that door but I need help."

Lyons was puzzled. He shook his head. "Well if you really want to, you can leave any time you like," he replied. "I'll be sorry to see you go, and I'm sure that the others will be as well."

Ashby smiled. "I wish it were that easy," he said, as he looked at the door. "Just leave, just like that."

"It is that easy," Lyons said. "Look, I'll show you." He walked over to the door, and opened it. "See, there's nothing to stop you, the door is open, so all you have to do is walk through."

Ashby went to the door, and looked out. As he had expected there was no clearing in the forest. Just the driveway, and the wall. He stepped back.

"So you've changed your mind about going, maybe," said Lyons. "But I'm puzzled, you talk of escape as though this were a prison."

Ashby nodded. "Well in some ways, ways that you wouldn't understand, it is a prison to me."

"Well there's the door, and it is open, so out you go."

Ashby looked out once again. He looked at Lyons. "It's no use, it won't help," he said. "It's still here, at the school, and more importantly it's still now."

Lyons was more puzzled than ever. "What do you mean?" he asked.

"Its 1890," said Ashby. "It's your time. It's not mine."

But clearly Lyons did not understand and why should he, Ashby thought. *I don't understand myself.* The whole story was too fantastic.

Ashby heaved a sigh. Yes it was a fantastic story, but he needed to tell it. He looked back at the entrance door. "I was born in nineteen eighty-six, ninety-six years from here and now," he started to explain. "My queen is Elizabeth the second. Your queen, Victoria, died in 1901, her son,

Edward became king and reigned until 1910. In 1914 we went to war. And again in 1939."

Lyons said nothing but heaved a sigh.

"On the 5th of April 2021, I was standing just on the other side of that door." He pointed to it and heaved a sigh. Lyons looked over to where he had pointed. Ashby shook his head. "It was just a door, nothing else. Standing in a clearing in the forest. There was none of this." Ashby waved his arms around him. "This building, the school, the boys, you, Dr Shutt. None of it existed. Just a door."

"Oh, come on Ashby, enough of this," Lyons said smiling. "I really haven't time for a story. Mind you the boys might enjoy it. They like ghost stories."

Chapter Nine
31st December 1890 –
This Is No Story

"This is no story," said Ashby. "I wish it was. Please hear me out. I'm not mad, although there are times when ...." He sighed and took a deep breath. "It just seems like a bad dream, a nightmare." He paused for a moment, wondering whether he should continue or not. "You know I had been warned, stay away from the door, that's what I was told. Stay away, but did I listen? Not at all. I started to play around. I can't believe I was so childish, so stupid. I knocked on the door, you know. Went right up to it and knocked. Open up I cried. And amazingly enough the door opened. I couldn't believe it."

"Who answered it? The matron I'm guessing," suggested Lyons.

"No, it wasn't the matron. Remember what I said, it wasn't anyone," replied Ashby. "It just opened. I foolishly walked through, going from the forest into this hallway, and in so doing I walked back one hundred and thirty-one years from 2021 to 1890."

Lyons heaved a sigh. He looked at Ashby. "So the door just happen to open and you walked through. Is that right?" He held up his hand. "No, don't answer that. But tell me this, what about your luggage? I mean where did that come from, if it didn't come from you? And don't forget your luggage arrived the day before you did."

Ashby shook his head, he had no answer.

"And another thing, everyone was expecting you, including old Daniel, and even the boys," Lyons continued. "How could that be? Answer me that."

Ashby had to admit that he had no answer. It was a complete mystery to him. "All I know is that I came through that door, from another time."

Lyons shook his head. "No, that cannot be," he said. "Logic tells us that it is not possible."

Ashby smiled. "You're right, I agree completely," he said. "And it should not be possible, but it happened just the way I said."

Lyons was become more and more exasperated. "Alright Ashby, let's say that it did happen, the way you said," he replied. "You came here, from one hundred and whatever years into the future, to our school. Just look at your clothes. It seems that fashions haven't changed for all of that time. They look as though they were bought just a few weeks ago in a London store."

Ashby looked down at his clothes. Oddly enough he hadn't even considered them before, but now he had to admit that the style was not the modern cut that he was used to. He looked at the clothes that Lyons was wearing. They were identical to his own. "I don't know, I don't understand," replied Ashby becoming agitated. "I don't know anything anymore. Nothing makes sense. But what I do know, is that I don't belong here, in this time. You've got to believe me."

"I would like to believe you, but it's difficult," said Lyons. He heaved a sigh. "There's just so much that states that your story just could not have happened."

"I don't belong here," Ashby insisted. "I don't care about the luggage, or the clothes, or even the letters."

"What about that photograph?" Lyons continued. "Taken fifteen years ago, in 1875?"

"What photograph?" Ashby asked, knowing full well what Lyons had in mind.

"You know the one I mean," said Lyons. "The one that I saw lying in your room surrounded by broken glass."

"Were you in my room?" Ashby asked angrily. "What were you doing? Spying on me?"

"David, I just came to see you," Lyons explained. "I knocked, but there was no answer. But then I noticed that the door wasn't closed properly. As I knocked once again the door opened. It was then that I saw the broken glass. I went in. Yes I know I shouldn't have, but the sight of all that glass, I thought maybe you had had an accident. Then I saw the photograph." He paused for a moment, and put his hand on Ashby's shoulder. "That was you wasn't it? It certainly looked like you, a younger version certainly, but there's no mistake, it is you. Someone has written your name across the photograph, and added a date. 12th September 1875."

Ashby took a deep breath. "Yes, yes, yes. It was me, but I don't understand it at all. The date just doesn't make any sense. It was taken ninety years before I was born. How is that possible?"

"David, have you ever considered that maybe you do belong here," Lyons said. "In this time 1890, and that the other time you speak about, 2021, is the real fantasy in your mind."

"No, you're wrong. That's just not right," Ashby protested, shaking his head. "You mention the date on the photograph, well the 12th September was the day I started as a teacher at Highgate School, the 12th September 2005."

"David, I'm only trying to help you. This is where you belong, face it. Everything fits," Lyons insisted. "The luggage, the letters, the photograph, everything. And don't forget you actually had the key to your trunk. It makes sense to me. At least as much sense as anything else. You must at least admit that it's a possibility, or at least it is as likely to be right, as your story is."

"It's not a story," protested Ashby. "It's the truth. I was born in nineteen sixty two. It was in 2021 that I foolishly walked through that door, and arrived here."

"Yes, David, that's what you say," replied Lyons. "But that makes no sense. A door, just a door, in a field. Admit it, it's a story isn't it? Besides so far everything seems to say different. So at least you must consider my suggestion."

Ashby shook his head. *Could it be,* he wondered. Was Lyons right? *Perhaps he was, and perhaps I am wrong.* Am I just imagining things? Perhaps I really do belong in this place, and this time. Perhaps that was the reality. Maybe 2021 was the fantasy.

Then he suddenly remembered something. "What about my books," he announced excitedly. "They will show a publication date, and then you'll have to admit I'm right."

"Alright," agreed Lyons. "Let us take a look."

Ashby rushed to his room, and grabbed four books. He hurried back to Lyons. "There we are," he said. "Take a look."

Lyons took hold of the first one, and opened it. He started to read "Pictures and

Royal Portraits, English and Scottish History. Written by Thomas Archer, and published in." He paused and looked at Ashby. "Published in 1880." He held out his hand. "Second book please."

Ashby handed him the second volume.

Lyons opened it, and once again began to read. "Ah, this is an interesting one. John Wisden's Cricketeers Almanack, 1879." He paused and once again looked at Ashby. "I thought you said you didn't play."

Things were not going well for Ashby.

"Next one, please," said Lyons holding out his hand.

Ashby placed the third book into Lyon's hand. "Ah, I love this book," Lyons said. "King Solomon's Mines, by H Rider Haggard. What a great story, published just a few years ago in 1885." He shook his head. "Any more?" he asked.

Ashby was becoming more and more despondent. He made no reply and simply handed Lyons the fourth, and final book.

Lyons smiled. "The great English Painters, written by Francis Downham," he read. He looked up at Ashby. "Published in 1886." He took a deep breath and heaved a sigh. "You know, considering these books are way over one hundred years old, they are in remarkable condition. You really have looked after them well."

Ashby shook his head. "This isn't right," he protested as he grabbed the book out of Lyons' hand, and quickly turned the pages. The year 1886 stared back at him. He let the book go, and watched it fall to the floor. "They are not my books I tell you. I've never seen them before in my life."

Lyons was fast losing patience. "Ashby, I don't know what game you are playing, but whatever it is, I don't like it, so please just stop." He looked at the four books that were now lying on the floor. "Those four books were in your trunk, your locked trunk." He paused once again. "Tell me who had the key to open that trunk?"

Ashby reluctantly agreed that the key had been in the pocket of his jacket.

"So how did it get there?" Lyons asked.

"I don't know," replied Ashby. "I just don't know."

"You do know, Ashby," replied Lyons. "You put it there. I don't know when, or where you were, but ....."

Ashby was shaking his head. "I didn't put it there," he protested.

"Then who did?" asked Lyons.

Ashby had to admit that it was a perfectly reasonable question, and he truly wished that he had a perfectly reasonable answer, but he didn't. "I don't know how it got there."

Lyons heaved a sigh. "I'm sorry but I can't waste any more time discussing it. I've other things to do with my time," he said. "I suggest you go back to your room, and have a lie down. I'll send Matron up to see you later, she'll give you something to help you relax." He paused and smiled. "Think about what I've said. Things will seem much better after a good sleep."

"I don't belong here, Donny," Ashby said almost in a whisper. "I'm telling you I'm from the year 2021. You must believe me."

"A good story but I have to go," replied Lyons. "There are arrangements to make for tonight. Great tale though." Lyons hurried away smiling.

Ashby watched him go. He had achieved nothing, and only appeared foolish. He looked back at the door, and tried the handle once again. The door remained closed.

* * *

Chapter Ten

31st December 1890 –

1st January 1891

Ashby returned to his room. So he had spoken to someone in the hope of understanding and help. Instead he had looked like a fool, and now doubted his own thoughts. His head was full of the things that Lyons had been saying. *Was it possible?* He wondered. Did he really belong in this place, and this time? Was 2021 nothing more than his imagination running wild? But was that actually possible? Could you really imagine something without having prior knowledge of it? No, of course you couldn't. *No, that isn't right,* he thought. *Authors do it all the time. Their stories are all from imagination.*

And yet the events that he spoke of were so vivid in his mind. Details of his birth and his references to the Monarchy, they weren't imagined. They were specific facts. How would he know of such things? And yet Lyons had sown doubts in his mind. He had to admit that his so-called facts were of no real value. They were, after all, just statements that he was unable to prove. Perhaps, they were merely figments of his imagination. In the same way as Robert Louis Stevenson imagined all manner of things, when he wrote about a Treasure Island.

Imagination, thought Ashby. *Nothing more than imagination.*

Ashby was very disturbed. He decided to thoroughly check his possessions. There must be something there to link him with 2021. He started with his jacket. He emptied the contents of his pockets on to the bed, and began to look through them.

He picked up his wallet, and opened it. The first thing he noticed was a ticket. London Street Tramways, 28th December 1890, Highgate West Hill to Hampstead. He pushed it to one side, and then he saw the letter. It was addressed to him, and was from the Sir Roger Cholmeley's School, Highgate, wishing him good fortune in his new position at The Lansdown School. The letter was dated 25th September 1890. "That cannot be," he said as he angrily tossed it aside.

Could it be that Lyons was correct? That he did belong in 1890? The evidence seemed overwhelming. It was there, right in front of him. Lyons words echoed through his mind, over and over. And yet still he could not accept it. The year 2021 was so real to him. The door that he had seen for so many years; the forest clearing; his grandfather; his warnings. The words were so strong in his mind, the vision of his grandfather so clear. Lyons must have been wrong. And yet ….

* * *

Ashby's thoughts were interrupted by a knock on his door. "Just a moment," he called out. He quickly gathered up the items covering his bed, and placed them in the bedside cabinet drawer.

He then went over to the door. True to his word Lyons had sent the Matron to see him.

"Mr. Lyons said that you were having problems sleeping," she said. "I have brought you something which will help."

Certainly he was having trouble sleeping, but a couple of tablets was not the answer. Ashby smiled. "Miss Bradley it's really very kind of you, but I'm alright," he said. "There's no need to make a fuss"

But Matron insisted. She placed a mug of herb tea on to the table. "It is catmint tea, it will help you sleep," she explained. "And take these tablets." She opened her hand and offered them to Ashby.

"What are they?" Ashby asked.

"Valerian," replied the Matron.

Ashby heaved a sigh. "Just leave them there," he said. "I'll take them later."

"Take them, now," the matron insisted, offering him the tablets once again.

Ashby knew that he was beaten, and reluctantly took them.

"Now drink the tea," Matron instructed.

Ashby realised that she was not going to leave until he had complied with her instructions. He began sipping the tea. After a few moments, he put the mug down. "There, I've taken it," he announced.

Matron looked at the mug. It was still half full. She picked it up, and handed it back to Ashby. "Drink it," she ordered. "All of it."

Ashby did her bidding, and drained the mug. He smiled at the Matron, and held out the empty mug for her to see. She smiled, stood up and walked to the door. "You know where I am if you need more tea."

Ashby nodded. "Oh I'll be sure to call on you."

* * *

Not long after the Matron had left, there was another knock on Ashby's door. It was Lyons. "Did the Matron come to see you?" he asked, as he walked into the room.

"Oh yes, she came," replied Ashby. "In fact it isn't that long since she left. She gave me a couple of tablets, Valerian."

"Well, let us hope that they help you," said Lyons.

Ashby sighed. "They won't help my problem."

"Oh no, we're not starting that again are we?" said Lyons shaking his head. "Look, it's nearly midnight. Fireworks, remember. Come on, let's go, the boys will be waiting."

Ashby nodded. "Okay, but I have to tell you I'm not a great lover of fireworks."

"Oh, they are just a bit of fun, and besides it's more for the boys, rather than us," said Lyons, leading Ashby out of the room, and down the stairs.

As they came down the stairs they could hear the sound of laughter coming from somewhere down in the hall. Then there was the sound of the clock striking the hour, followed by calls of "happy New Year".

As the final stroke of midnight sounded, the first rocket shot into the sky. It exploded releasing dozens of sparkling lights. Then squibs, crackers, began to hiss, and explode into showers of colour. And more rockets shot into the air. Catherine wheels whirled, and bomb shells boomed loudly.

* * *

All too soon the firework display was over. And the boys were sent, albeit reluctantly, to their beds. Lyons and Ashby went back upstairs.

"Well Ashby, that's that. One year ends, and a new one begins," said Lyons. "I wonder what kind of year it will be." He smiled. "You get a good rest," he said, as he left Ashby at his door. "I'll see you in the morning, but not too early. Good night" He laughed, gave a wave, and continued along the landing to his room.

Ashby watched him go, and then went into his room.

Yes I wonder what kind of a year it will be, murmured Ashby. *Will I still be here, or will I return to my time?* He closed the door. He suddenly thought of his friends and family. In 2021 he had a wife, and a family, and many friends. *Funny,* he thought, *I haven't given them a thought since I've been here at Lansdown.*

He smiled, at last he had a link to 2021, but once again he realised that he could not prove anything. So it was unlikely that Lyons would believe him. But nonetheless he had a family, a family who, perhaps, must be wondering where he was. Perhaps there were already people searching for him right now. He smiled, pleased at the thought. Then he realised that there was no chance that they would ever find him. Not in the present circumstances. Then another unwelcome thought came into his mind. *Maybe they weren't real after all. Maybe they were merely imagined, like everything else,* he thought. *Perhaps, that's the reason I haven't given them any thought before.*

Ashby no longer knew truth from fantasy. He was no longer sure of what was right, and what was wrong. What was real, and what was imagined.

* * *

There were more calls of Happy New Year. Then someone cried out, "Good night everyone." Then there was silence. The only sound was the ticking of the clock on the stairs.

It was just twenty minutes into the New Year when Miss Bradley was aroused by the smell of smoke, and the sound of crackling timbers. She got up, and went down the stairs. As she reached the hallway she saw smoke coming from a small kitchen area. She ran back up the staircase, and rang the alarm bell.

At the sound of the alarm, Ashby got up, and quickly dressed. He hurried from his room, meeting up with several of the teachers on the landing where Miss Bradley was waiting. She explained that there was a fire in the small kitchen area on the ground floor. Within a very short time the fire had taken hold and was beginning to spread to the curtaining close by. Within minutes the flames were shooting high, and attacking the ceiling timbers. Smoke billowed upwards, through the floor structure, into the dormitories on the floor above, where the children were sleeping, unaware of the danger.

"We must get the boys out of the dormitories," said Lyons. "Alec you go to room nine, I'll take room ten."

Alec Aldridge, made his way up the staircase, from the outside, to the dormitory at the top of the landing. The door would not open. Aldridge pushed hard, and eventually forced his way into the dormitory. The room was already full of smoke. He hurried over to the door on to the first floor landing, but was driven back by the dense smoke coming up from the staircase. He rushed back to the external staircase, calling to the boys to follow him.

Mr. Lyons attempted to ascend a staircase leading to one of the other dormitories but was stopped for a time by a dense and pungent cloud of smoke. By crawling on his hands and knees he reached the door of the dormitory, and led the boys out to safety.

Meanwhile, Ashby had hurried down the stairs. As he reached the hallway the moonlight streaming through a window showed a figure running towards the back door. Ashby was sure that it was Wyndham. But why was he there, he had been dismissed

The man suddenly stopped, and glanced around. He saw Ashby looking at him. He hurriedly continued along the corridor. Ashby began to follow, but the fire quickly took hold, and soon the whole of the east wing was alight.

The night sky was suddenly lit up for miles around by the flames rising high into the air. The smell of acrid smoke billowing was soon overpowering. Ashby, overcome by fumes, staggered and fell. As he did so part of the ceiling gave way and knocked him to the ground. Badly burnt, Ashby began dragging himself along the corridor. He could hear several people shouting, crying for help. Some were calling his name. Desperate to escape the inferno, he suddenly heard the voice of his grandfather. "Don't you ever go near it," his grandfather had said, pointing to the door "There's danger."

How he wished he had heeded those words.

With the fire raging behind him, and his strength failing, Ashby continued to drag himself along the corridor towards the main entrance door. He noticed that the door was open. He looked through the door opening. The gravelled driveway had gone, so too was the school wall. And he could see the clearing in the forest. He could also see the open field and the trees that he remembered from what seemed so long ago. Now he can get away he murmured, and he pulled himself out of the building. There was no sound, except for the cries for help coming from beyond the door. He pulled himself further and further until he had no more strength.

A few minutes later he stopped, and turned to look towards the building. There was no sign of a building, or of a fire. All he could see was a door, an ordinary door. The cries had ceased, and the only sound he could hear was his grandfather's warning.

He took a deep breath, and lay down, the grass was cool against his face.

Exhausted, he closed his eyes. A few minutes later and he was dead. He had escaped at last. He was now finally free.

* * *

Chapter Eleven
26th June 2021

The morning had threatened rain, but the sun was now shining brightly in a clear blue sky. A good day for a brisk walk with his dog, Gyp, Richard Bates thought. Suddenly the dog ran off. A rabbit, Richard guessed, and then he smiled. There was no way that the dog would catch it, no way at all. Then Richard noticed that the dog had stopped and was sniffing at something on the ground. "He's found something, surely not the rabbit," Richard said to no one in particular, as he walked over to the dog.

David Ashby's body was lying in the undergrowth, forty feet from an old door. He was quite dead, and had been badly burnt.

Richard took his mobile phone out of his pocket and dialled 999. The emergency services arrived five minutes later, and soon the area was a hive of activity.

Several people were hovering around, taking photographs, and measurements. Crime scene tape had been placed into position. Close by police vehicles were lined up, and over to one side stood an ambulance.

Richard looked back at the scene. He shook his head, wondering what was actually happening. He sighed. *Probably all be on the six o'clock news,* he thought. He looked around. "Gyp, he called. "Where are you? Come on boy, let's go."

The dog came running up, tail wagging. Richard bent down and re-secured the lead. "Come on, let's go home, for dinner shall we?" The dog gave an enthusiastic bark.

Richard took one last look over to the police activity, and walked on. A few yards from the scene he saw the door. Just a door, an ordinary door …..

He wondered how it had got there, and where the rest of the building was.

* * *

A police officer was leaning over the body. He stood up, he was holding a wallet. "Ashby," he said. "That's his name, sergeant. "Ashby. David Ashby"

"Ashby did you say?" said the Sergeant. "That name sounds familiar."

"Isn't he the one who disappeared a couple of months back?" said the officer.

"I think so," agreed the Sergeant.

"He's badly burnt, sir," the officer continued. "The question is how did he get burnt?"

The Sergeant looked down at the body, and shook his head. "I don't understand it at all," he replied. "There's no signs of there having been a fire close by." He paused and looked around. "No, nothing. Not a thing."

"Nothing, except for that," said the officer pointing.

The Sergeant looked in the direction indicated. Approximately forty feet away there was an old door. "Well, forensics will be here soon. They'll find out, bet your life."

The officer smiled. "Guess so." He looked back at the body. "You know, Sergeant, I'm not an expert or anything, but do you notice anything odd about his clothes?"

The Sergeant started to laugh. "Apart from being burnt to a cinder you mean?"

"I'm talking about the style", explained the constable. "His clothes look pretty ancient to me, fifty or sixty years old maybe."

The sergeant looked closer. "You know, I see what you mean, and you're right. They're the sort of clothes my old grand dad used to wear."

"Well, we must be wrong," said the constable. "I mean it just can't be can it?"

The Sergeant nodded. "Anything else in that wallet?" he asked.

The constable looked back at the wallet. "There's this," he replied handing a piece of paper to the Sergeant. "That don't make any sense either."

The Sergeant looked at the paper. "It's a newspaper cutting," he said hesitantly. "It's dated 3 January 1891, and it's all about a fire at a school."

"Strange." said the constable. He looked at the body. "Maybe he was connected to it in some way."

"How'd you mean?" asked the Sergeant.

"Oh, I don't know," said the Constable. "Maybe one of his ancestors was one of the teachers, or maybe one of the pupils. Who knows?"

Who indeed, the Sergeant wondered. "Either way it doesn't help us. We still don't know how he got burnt so badly do we?"

"No sir," replied the constable, as he continued searching for any clue as to how Ashby had died. "Hey, Sergeant, where was that school?"

"School?" repeated the Sergeant. "You mean that one that burnt down? The one in the newspaper cutting?"

"That's right Sergeant," said the Constable. "Was it Hampstead, by any chance?"

"Yes, it was, Hampstead," the Sergeant replied. "Why?"

"Thought so," said the constable. "Oddly enough, I found this in his coat." He held up a small piece of paper. "It's a ticket, a tram ticket. A single from Highgate to Hampstead. Looks like he was recently there."

"Well, perhaps he went to see the spot where that school used to be," suggested the Sergeant. "Except of course we haven't had trams for sixty years or more."

"1952 was the year the last London tram operated," said the Constable. "1952." He looked at the ticket. "The date on this here ticket, is 28th December 1890."

"1890, did you say?" replied the Sergeant. "Must be a typing error, that's all."

"I guess you're right, sir," said the Constable. "But we'll never know will we?"

"That's right, we'll never know," said the Sergeant. "Come on, we've a lot to do, so get on with it."

"Yes sir," said the constable.

* * *

So what would you do? You are walking in the countryside, and you come across a door standing in a clearing. Just a solitary timber door and frame, standing in a field, or a clearing in the forest .... Just a door .... Just an ordinary door .... and that's all. There are no other signs of a building. What do you think? What goes through your mind? Do you just ignore it and walk by, or are you mischievous, playful. Do you go up to it and knock.

Printed in Great Britain
by Amazon

26500448R00089